To James,
Happy _____ '97
Love _____,
Fiona + Ali
x

To my son, Franek

BAREFOOT BEGINNERS

An imprint of Barefoot Books Ltd

PO Box 95, Kingswood, Bristol BS15 5BH

Copyright © 1996 by Tomek Bogacki

Designed by Monika Keano

First published in the United States of America in 1996 by Farrar, Straus & Giroux

This edition first published in the United Kingdom in 1997 by Barefoot Books

Printed and bound in Spain

ISBN: 1 901223 56 6

Tomek Bogacki

Cat and Mouse

BAREFOOT BEGINNERS

BATH

Mother Mouse was teaching her children
about the world . . . But not all of them.
One little mouse was not paying attention.
She was curious about everything.

Mother Cat was teaching her children
about the world, too. But one little
cat was not paying attention. He was
curious, too.

The curious little mouse and the curious little cat met in the green meadow.

"I have never seen an animal so different from me," said the mouse.

"*I* have never seen an animal so different from *me*," said the cat.

The little mouse made a terrifying face.
"Are you afraid of me?" she asked.
"No!" said the cat.

The little cat made himself as big and
as scary as he could.
"Are you afraid of *me*?" he asked.
"No!" said the mouse.

So the little mouse and the little
cat began to play.

They rolled down the hill.

They swung from a tree.

They played and played . . .

. . . until the sun went down.

"Come home, come home, little mouse,"
called Mother Mouse. "It is getting dark."

"Come home, come home, little cat,"
called Mother Cat. "It is getting late."

"I have never had so much fun!" the little
mouse said to her sisters.
"I played with a cat!"
"How could you have fun with a cat?" they
asked.

"I made friends with a mouse," the little cat
said to his brothers.
"I have never had so much fun."
"How could you be friends with a mouse?"
they asked.

Then the other little mice and the other little cats got curious, too. The very next day they all met in the green meadow . . .

. . . and they played and played until
their mothers called them home.